PEACOCK AND SKETCH

BY
ALLAN PETERKIN, MD

ILLUSTRATED BY
SANDHYA PRABHAT

Magination Press • Washington, DC •
American Psychological Association

For Audrey, who told me so many wonderful stories—AP

Magination Press is a registered trademark of the American Psychological Association. Order books at maginationpress.org, or call 1-800-374-2721.
Book design by Rachel Ross
Printed by Phoenix Color, Hagerstown, MD

Library of Congress Cataloging-in-Publication Data
Names: Peterkin, Allan, author. | Prabhat, Sandhya, illustrator.
Title: Peacock and Sketch / by Allan Peterkin ; illustrations by Sandhya Prabhat.
Description: [Washington, D.C.]: Magination Press, an imprint of the American Psychological Association, 2021. | Summary: A fame-seeking peacock discovers the fleeting nature of social stardom and the importance of real-world friendship. Includes note to parents on the benefits and risks of social media and how fame cannot replace friendship.
Identifiers: LCCN 2021006590 (print) | LCCN 2021006591 (ebook) | ISBN 9781433832796 (hardback) | ISBN 9781433837555 (ebook)
Subjects: CYAC: Peacocks—Fiction. | Fame—Fiction. | Friendship—Fiction. | Social media—Fiction.
Classification: LCC PZ7.P4415455 Pe 2021 (print) | LCC PZ7.P4415455 (ebook) | DDC [E]—dc23
LC record available at https://lccn.loc.gov/2021006590
LC ebook record available at https://lccn.loc.gov/2021006591

Manufactured in the United States of America
10 9 8 7 6 5 4 3 2 1

PEACOCK was the only peacock in the whole zoo, and he liked it that way.

When he unfurled
his feathers, the visitors
OoOoHED
and AAAHED.

They took endless photos.

And boy, did Peacock know
how to pose.

One little girl called Sketch came almost every day.

Instead of taking pictures, Sketch drew in a little notebook

VERRRRY SLOWWWLY.

She liked watching Peacock show off his beautiful tail feathers.

But on quiet days, he was bored and lonely sitting in his pen, all by himself.

On those days, she would just tell him stories in a soft voice.

NOBODY had ever done that before.

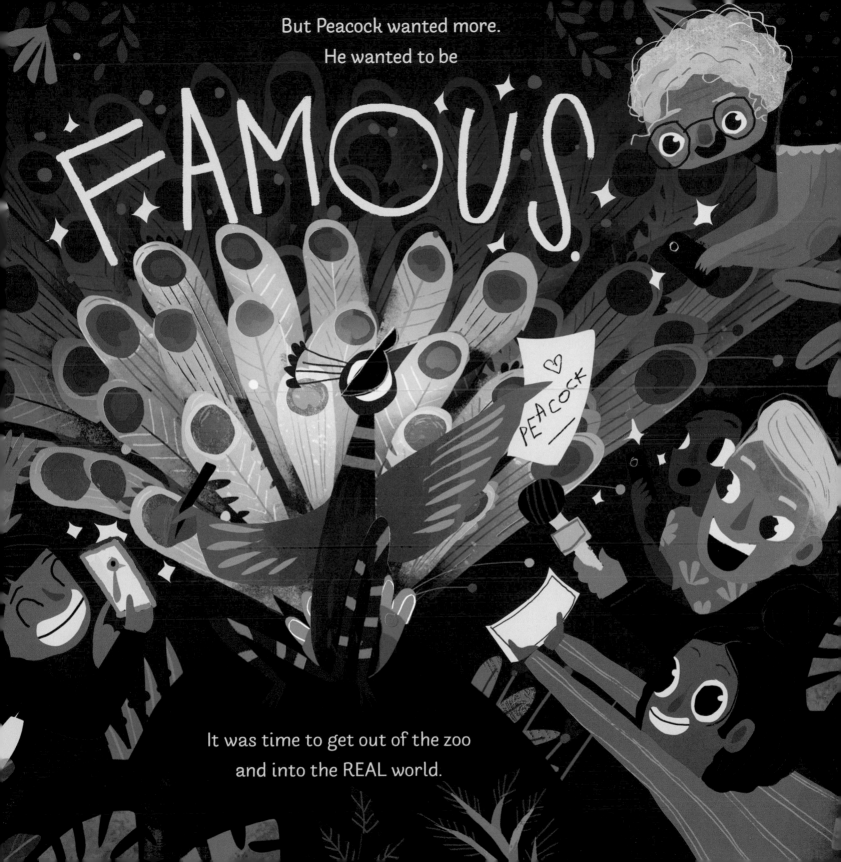

One day a school bus full of children arrived.
It was Sketch's class!

This was Peacock's BIG chance.

When no one was looking, he flew out of his coop and landed on the roof of the school bus.

SCHOOL BUS

Sketch saw him jump but didn't say a word.

As the bus hit the road, Peacock fanned his feathers all the way out.

He strutted and STRETCHED. And puffed and posed.

All the cars honked and honked.
A car with a flashing red light came toward the bus.

"This is FANTASTIC!"
thought Peacock.

CHOOL BUS

"But I'd better not
get caught."

Peacock flew off the bus and over to an old building.
He peered inside and rolled his eyes.
How could the real world be so QUIET?

He walked inside, full-feathered.

Everyone started to OOOoOH and AAAAH

and SNAP SNAP SNAP

Until a lady with a small gray nest
on her head ruined his moment.

Peacock flew up to the roof of a building with a big ledge.

"All this attention is tiring!
I really need my afternoon nap,"
he thought to himself.

Peacock made himself comfortable and took a short snooze. **ZZZZZZ**.

Peacock was soon awakened by
SNAP SNAP SNAPS
and loud shouting from
down below.
He was very sleepy and
teetered awfully close to the edge.

Suddenly he recognized a friendly voice.
Sketch was there, waving!
"Peacock, be careful. You've seen the world.
Now please go back HOME!"

Peacock flew down in swooping circles
and landed on the top of a big truck.

THUMP!

The truck started to move
in the direction of the zoo.

Peacock fanned out his feathers for all his new fans.

SHOWTIME!

When they finally got to the zoo,

Peacock's neck hurt from posing.

His eyes hurt from the flashes.

His ears hurt from the sirens.

Even his feathers were sore!

FAME could be a real bother.

It was getting dark and he hadn't eaten a thing all day.

He was kind of glad to be

HOME.

After his big adventure,
Peacock got his wish.
He was

FAMOUS.

Some reporters
even started
calling him

Selfie
the
Peacock

People lined up around his
pen for a selfie with Selfie.

SNAP! SNAP! SNAP!

Newspapers all over the world wrote about his

ROUD PEACOCK PARADE

Then disaster struck.

By the end of the summer,
Peacock's tail feathers fell out.

Every single one!

NO ONE remembered him.

And

NOBODY

came to visit.

Except for one little girl.

Sketch brought a finished picture from
when she had first met Peacock.

He couldn't believe his eyes.

Lots of people had LOOKED at him
when he was showing off.

But Sketch had **SEEN** how he felt.

"How did she know?" he wondered.

Sketch kept coming,

RAIN
_or_
SHINE.

She told Peacock not to worry about losing his feathers. That molting was just a normal part of growing up. She knew a lot about birds.

Peacock sat quietly.
He listened closely and
looked at her the way
she looked at him.

He liked Sketch's smile.
And her freckles.
And the way she
held her pencil.

Sketch's drawings still
took a long time.
But each picture was
ONE OF A KIND.

And Peacock definitely had
A FAVORITE.

READER'S NOTE

Children are gravitating to social media at younger and younger ages. Most kids have smartphones, and many spend six or more hours every day using them. Immediate gratification from texts and images can replace conversations, storytelling, and real human contact. Children may not go inward to tap their imaginations or go outside to play when they're bored. Social media can distract, disrupt sleep, over-stimulate, and reduce attention spans, social skills, and language skills, both inside and outside of the classroom.

Appearance is especially valued on social media platforms. Kids learn to pose and objectify themselves and others, leading to envy, FOMO (fear of missing out), and concerns around body image, popularity, and self-esteem. Everybody else seems perfect in this curated, edited, photo-shopped universe, but no one gets to be vulnerable or authentic.

Experts talk about the "Three Cs" in social media, which are a good framework for parents to use when talking to their children about the benefits and risks of social media:

- CONTENT: Is what's posted age-appropriate? Truthful? Helpful? What information should never be shared? How does your child feel after accessing specific images and messages? Invite them to discuss anything that makes then uncomfortable.

- CONTACT: Is it safe to connect with people you don't really know? What might the risks be? Can your child see beyond glossy images or clever posts and think about a real person with feelings on the other end? Kids need to be reminded that all these anonymous followers are not actual friends.

- CONDUCT: This concerns courtesy, ethical behavior, and empathy. Words can hurt if they lead to judgment, humiliation, and bullying. Parents can give their own examples of deciding to wait and reflect instead of replying impulsively or angrily to a message that bothered them.

Parents reading *Peacock and Sketch* can explore with their children how online connections can be fun and teach you lots of things about the world and human nature. But they can use the story to emphasize that a real friend loves the real you, even when you don't look or feel so great, and shows up in person when things get tough. Fame can't replace friendship.

Allan Peterkin, MD, is a physician and writer. He is a professor of psychiatry and family medicine and head of the Program in Health, Arts, and Humanities at the University of Toronto. Dr. Peterkin is the author of several children's books, including *Chill, The Flyaway Blanket,* and *The Dream Journal.* He lives in Toronto, Canada.